Samuel Hawkins Marshall Byers

The Happy Isles

And Other Poems

Samuel Hawkins Marshall Byers

The Happy Isles
And Other Poems

ISBN/EAN: 9783337407711

Printed in Europe, USA, Canada, Australia, Japan

Cover: Foto ©Andreas Hilbeck / pixelio.de

More available books at **www.hansebooks.com**

THE HAPPY ISLES,

AND

OTHER POEMS.

S. H M BYERS.

———◆—◆—◆———

NEW YORK:

CHARLES L. WEBSTER & CO.

1891.

Press of
JENKINS & McCOWAN,
224 Centre St., N. Y.

A FEW of the poems in this volume were first printed in magazines, and some were contained in a previous volume, but many appear now for the first time.

TO MY WIFE

THIS LITTLE VOLUME IS LOVINGLY
INSCRIBED.

CONTENTS.

X   *CONTENTS.*

THE HAPPY ISLES.

ONCE on a time, in beauteous Paradise,
Two angels wandered at the even-tide,
Beneath a splendor of celestial skies,
With banks of violets on every side.
And to their ears, came ever far and wide,
Soft notes of flutes, voluptuous melodies,
That mortals, hearing, had in rapture died.
So soft they came, the murmuring of the seas
Was stilled, to listen to their ecstasies.

And while they wandered, all their senses
    filled
With the sweet thought to be forever young,
All things a joy, and every longing stilled,
With not a heart by any sorrow wrung,
And life a song to be forever sung, —
A thought came o'er them like a sacred spell,
Of loved and left, far other scenes among,

Where no dear heart might ever go, to tell
How sweet is death, and how all things are
    well.

Then one did ask what loveliest thing there
    was,
That was most fair of anything on earth,
Of lovely flower, or eglantine, or rose,
Or tree, or thing of most surpassing worth,
And beauteous even from its very birth, —
Be it of groves, or seas, of human kind, or
    skies,
Or songs of winds, of sadness, or of mirth, —
What loveliest thing of all that ever dies,
Were fittest first to be in Paradise.

One said a nightingale, and one the gleam
Of summer sunset by some constant sea, —
And one, sweet apple-blooms that fall and
    seem
Wind-kissed, and lulled into an ecstasy
Of odorous death, if such a thing there be.
And others said, for many hastened near,
The loveliest thing in all the world to see,

Surpassing all, to heaven and earth most dear,
By angels welcomed, is a sorrowing tear.

One said the fragrance of a summer rose,
And one the melody of flutes at eve,
Or else the music of a brook that flows,
Murmuring farewell, and yet doth never
  leave, —
And some said moonlight nights that weave
In every soul sweet phantasies so deep
That mortals may of immortality conceive,
Nor longer wish their little lives to keep
From that sweet death which some of them
  call sleep.

But one there came, of others all the first,
And laid his hand upon a little child,
And quick there seemed a radiance to burst
About his face, ineffable and mild.
" *This* is the loveliest," he said, and smiled.
" Surpassing this, or lovelier, there is none, —
Rose-leaf of beauty, mortal undefiled.
The pearly gates no soul hath ever won,
That was not like unto this little one."

Then children came, and laid sweet baskets
    down,
Rose - leaf and violet, and every flower of
    worth,
And odorous herbs, and many a wreath and
    crown,
While in their midst stood one of mortal
    birth,
Herself more fair than any flower of earth.
Oh ! beauteous one, — oh ! face more perfect
    grown,
Though all unchanged, more beautiful thou
    art, —
E'en in thy angelhood, we still had known
Our heart-sweet lost — our loved, our very
    own.

Was it a vision that I saw her there,
Her face all gleaming in the light of His,
The sunlight shining on her sweet, brown
    hair,
That ever had been my delight to kiss,
In the old days, when seeing her was bliss?
It must have been — and if such things there
    be,

In fleeting visions of an hour like this,
What an Elysium the soul must see
In the sweet joys of an eternity !

'T is but a year — but little more, since she
And I were laughing by this beauteous lake;
There is the path, and there the little tree
I used to bend close to the ground, and make
A springing seat — 't was easy for her sake.
There, too, the grove, of Nidelbad the pearl,
The beechen trees no winds could ever break,
The cedars, bending like some plumèd earl
To her I loved, the little, laughing girl.

There are the Alps — there they will ever
    be, —
A thousand years will make no change in
    them,
Though rivers fail, and all the mighty sea,
Still they will wear their gracious diadem,
. Storm and the clouds their snowy mantles
    hem,
And they will shine as they have shone of
    old —

Their tops aflame, as on some evening, when
We watched the sun their palaces unfold, —
The sapphire roofs — the colonnades of gold.

And Zürich lake! thy waters ever will
Be dearer far than other scenes to me,
For I have wandered by thy shores until
My very being seemed akin to thee.
Each bank I knew, and every brook and
    tree,
Each vine-clad hill, and every hamlet fair,
And more I loved thee every day, that she
Was born to us amid a scene so rare, —
My heart will be forever turning there.

Forever turning to that beauteous scene,
Where she and I, the happy years agone,
Looked on the hills and the blue lake be-
    tween,
The blushing mountains in the dim beyond,
The ice-built palaces, and rocks whereon
A thousand years the frost-king travelleth,
Where the red sun, at evening and at dawn,

Spreads all in gold, as with a fairy's breath.
We looked and dreamed, but never dreamed
of death.

And it is done! One morn, the little bird
That waited ever at her window-pane
For some dear crumb, or for some dearer
word,
Plumed its sweet breast, and waited there in
vain.
Sweet heart! dear soul! she without any
stain,
Too pure for earth, born of far fairer skies,
Thoughtless of death, of darkness, or of pain,
Looking on us as if with other eyes,
Let go our hands and passed to Paradise.

With gentle hands, and gentle prayers, we
laid
Her body where the violets do blow;
· And if sometimes they should be thought to
fade,
With our warm tears we 'll water them, and so
For love of her, they will forever grow.

And many days, with broken hearts, we said,
" Could one return, or could we only know
She liveth yet, whom we have thus called
    dead,
Our souls in this might still be comforted."

And days and nights, we waited for a sign,
Praying and hoping she might linger there,
That word or look might lessen death's re-
    pine,
One single word might lighten our despair —
Might make the yoke more possible to bear.
We sought of silence — there was answer
    none,
We sought of moonlight, and of earth and
    air, —
There was no answer. Would she never come
One moment back, and strike all doubting
    dumb ?

And longing thus, as once I wept alone,
With heart bowed down, and face all wet
    with tears,
i felt her presence — felt my very own, —

And in that moment was the bliss of years.
Gone were my doubts, and gone were all my
  fears.
No dream was it — no phantasy could be
So like to her — the very thought endears.
It was no dream, that vision sweet — I see
Her dear form yet, and feel her kissing me.

One moment only, and one sweet embrace —
I felt her warm arms resting on my breast —
Her soft, warm cheek I felt against my face.
A thousand times I 'd put that head to rest,
Those little hands a thousand times caressed.
Dear eyes, sweet eyes! I know their tender
  gleam,
How oft their look some sorrowing heart hath
  blessed —
Dearer this night, than they did ever seem,
Dear one I love, I know it was no dream.

'T was but a moment, but that moment was
Rich in significance of things that are :
As some faint light behind the hill-top shows
The coming moon and her attendant star,

So with new eyes I saw, and from afar
Heard sweetest tones, and in the rosy West
Where they had left the golden gates ajar,
That she might come to give my spirit rest,
I looked and saw the Islands of the Blest.

Or dream, or waking, I may never know,
Alike the joy, no words may ever tell, —
I saw the isles where roses ever blow,
I saw the shores where bright seas ever
        swell —
It was the land where the blest spirits dwell.
I saw fair barks, by angels piloted
O'er roseate seas that only rose and fell
To notes of flutes, that thus were hallowèd,
While silver moons shed soft light overhead.

I saw the gardens of the happy Blest, —
The lotus-blooms, and golden asphodel,
And flowering shrubs angelic hands had
        dressed,
Red-berried ash, and the sweet mountain bell,
And thornless rose that doth forever smell,
And lilies fair, and waters all in tune

With odorous winds that came like fairy spell
Out of the night, to cool the parchèd noon,
And make the year a never-ending June.

I saw the fields that are forever green,
And purple hills that melt into the sea,
The thousand brooks that sing their way
     between,
One and a part of His great minstrelsy.
Not far away that happy sea may be,
Not far those sails by rapturous breezes bent,
With mortal eyes, at times, we almost see,
So near they are to our own firmament —
The Blessed Isles, where all men are content.

Gone is the vision of that blessed hour,
Like to some dream that with the morn is
     flown.
I saw the Isles, and every tree and flower
Melt and grow dim, as when a cloud is blown
. Across a moon that had that moment shone.
But as that moon and all her star-lit train,
Will still shine on, when the dark cloud is
     gone,

So will the clouds that hide my vision wane,
And I shall see the Blessed Isles again.

Shall ever think how very thin the veil
That floats at times betwixt myself and her,
Like mist of morn, or like some dewy sail, —
Ethereal cloud — so vapor-like, as 't were
A touch of wind, a gentle breath, might stir
Its shining folds — and I again should see,
Spread out like gold, as in my vision fair,
The Happy Isles, the far-off shining sea,
And her I loved, waiting to welcome me.

So I shall walk as now the earth along,
Dearer to me for one that has been here,
Nor shall the way seem very dark or long
To those Blest Isles whose confines do ap-
        pear.
And if, sometimes, in fancy I should hear
A dear, soft voice, or some light footstep's
        tread,
I shall be sure that she is very near,
And, thinking so, be gently comforted,
And live and love, as by her spirit led.

And many times my hand in hers will be,
And we will walk by pleasant ways alone,
And I shall look into her face, and see
The dearest eyes that ever yet have shone —
And cheeks more sweet than any roses
 blown.
And when, sometimes, light song and pleas-
 antry
Fill every heart but mine, to silence grown,
They will not know that, at that moment, she
Sits by my side and keeps me company.

SHERMAN'S MARCH TO THE SEA.

OUR camp-fires shone bright on the mount-
    ains,
    That frowned on the river below,
While we stood by our guns in the morning,
    And eagerly watched for the foe ;
When a rider came out from the darkness
    That hung over mountain and tree,
And shouted " Boys, up and be ready !
    For Sherman will march to the sea! "

Then cheer upon cheer for bold Sherman
    Went up from each valley and glen,
And the bugles re-echoed the music
    That came from the lips of the men ;
For we knew that the stars in our banner
    More bright in their splendor would be,
And that blessings from Northland would
      greet us,
    When Sherman marched down to the sea.

Then forward, boys! forward to battle!
 We marched on our perilous way,
And we stormed the wild hills of Resaca—
 God bless those who fell on that day!
Then Kenesaw, dark in its glory,
 Frowned down on the flag of the free;
But the East and the West bore our standards
 And Sherman marched on to the sea.

Still onward we pressed, till our banners
 Swept out from Atlanta's grim walls,
And the blood of the patriot dampened
 The soil where the rebel flag falls.
Yet we paused not to weep for the fallen,
 Who sleep by each river and tree,
But we twined them a wreath of the laurel,
 And Sherman marched on to the sea.

O! proud was our army that morning,
 That stood where the pine darkly towers,
When Sherman said, " Boys, you are weary;
 To-day fair Savannah is ours."

Then sang we a song for our chieftain,
   That echoed o'er river and lea,
And the stars in our banner shone brighter,
   When Sherman marched down to the sea.

THE BALLAD OF COLUMBUS.

IT was fourteen hundred and ninety-two,
  The close of the New Year's day,
When the armies of Catholic Ferdinand,
The flower of all the Spanish land,
  At the siege of Granada lay.

Ten thousand foot and ten thousand horse
  And ten thousand men with bows
Were on the left, and as many more
Had stormed close up to the city's door,
  Where the Darro River flows.

And the king held levee, for on that day
  Great news had come to court—
How on the morrow the town would yield,
And the flag of Spain, with the yellow field,
  Would float from the Moorish fort.

There were princely nobles and high grandees
  That night in the royal tent;

And the beautiful queen with the golden hair
And shining armor and sword was there—
  On the king's right arm she leant.

It was nine, and the old Alhambra bells
  Tolled out on the moonlit air;
And over the battlements far there came
The murmuring sound of Allah's name,
  And the Moorish troops at prayer.

"Hark!" said the king, as he heard the
    sound,
  "Hark, hark! to you bell's refrain—
Five hundred years it has called the Moor;
This night, and 'twill call him nevermore—
  To-morrow 'twill ring for Spain!"

Then spake a guest at the king's right hand:
  "To-morrow the end will be;
Hast thou not said, when the war is done
And the Christ flag floats o'er the Moslem
    one,
  Thou wouldst keep thy promise to me?

"Thou wouldst give me ships, and wouldst
    give me men
Who would dare to follow me?
Help thou this night with thy royal hand,
And I'll make thee king of a new-found land
    And king of a new-found sea.

"For the world is round, and a ship may sail
    Straight on with the setting sun,
Beyond Atlantis a thousand miles,
Beyond the peaks of the golden isles,
    To the Ophir of Solomon.

"So I'll find new roads to the golden isles,
    To the gardens that bloom alway,
To the treasure-quarries of Ispahan,
The sunlit hills of the mighty Khan,
    And the wonders of far Cathay.

"And gold I'll bring from the islands fair,
    And riches of palm and fir
Thou shalt have, my king; and the lords of
        Spain
Shall march with the Christ flag once again,
    And rescue the Sepulchre."

But the nobles smiled and the prelates
    sneered,
  With many a scornful fling;
" Had not the wisest already said
It was but the scheme of an empty head,
  And no fit thing for a king ?

" And were it true that the world is round,
  And not like an endless plain,
Were our good king's vessels the seas to ride
Adown the slope of the world's great side,
  How would they get up again ?'

" And the land of the fabled antipodes
  Was a wonderful land to see,
Where people stand with their heads on the
    ground,
And their feet in the air, while the world
    spins round "—
And they all laughed merrily.

But the king laughed not, though he scarce
    believed
  The things that his ears had heard;

And he thought full long of the promise fair,
And he knew that the day and the hour were
    there,
  If a king were to keep his word.

So he said, "For a while, for a little while,
  Let it bide, for the cost is great;"
But the guest replied: "Nay, seven years
I have waited on with my hopes and fears;
  And soon it will be too late."

Then spake the queen, "Be it done for me.
  Here are jewels for woe or weal;"
And she took the gems from her shining hair,
And the priceless pearls she was wont to
    wear,
  And she said, "For my own Castile."

  *   *   *   *   *   *   *

There were three ships sailing from Palos
  town,
  Ere the noon of a summer's day,
And the people looked at the ships and said,
"God pity their souls, for they all are dead;"
  But the ships went down the bay.

And an east wind blew, and the convent bells
   Rang out in sweet accord,
And the master stood on the deck and cried,
"We sail in the name of the Crucified,
   With the flag of Christ our Lord!"

They were ten days out when a storm wind
     blew—
   Ten days from the coast of Spain—
And the sailors shrived each other and said,
"God help us now, or we all are dead!
   We shall never see land again."

They were twelve days out when an ocean
     rock
   Burst forth in a sea of fire,
As if each peak and each lava cliff
Of the red-hot sides of Teneriffe,
   Were a sea-king's funeral pyre.

And the sailors crossed themselves and said,
   "Alas, for the day we swore
To follow a reckless adventurer—
Though it be at last to the Sepulchre—
   In search of an unknown shore."

And they spoke of the terror that lay be-
tween,
Of the hurricanes born of hell,
Of the sunless seas that forever roar,
Where the moon had perished long years
before,
When an evil spirit fell.

And ever the winds blew west, blew west,
And the ships blew over the main.
"They are cursed winds," the mariners said,
"That blow us forever ahead—ahead ;
They will never blow back to Spain."

But the master cited the Holy Writ;
And he told of a vision fair,
How a shining angel would show the way
To the Indus isles and the sweet Cathay,
And he "knew they were almost there."

But a sea-calm came, and the ships stood still,
And the sails drooped idle and low,
And a seaweed covered the vasty deep
As darkness covers a world in sleep,
And they feared for the rocks below.

It was twelve that night when a breeze
    sprang fresh,
  As if from a land close by,
And the sailors whispered each other and said,
"God only knows what next is ahead—
  Or if to-morrow we die."

It was two by the clock on the ship next
    morn,
  And breathless the sailors stand,
With eyes strained into the starless night,
When, lo! there's a cry of "A light, a light!"
  And a shout of "The land, the land!"

There were weeping eyes, there were press-
    ing hands,
  Till the dawn of that blessed day;
When the admiral, followed by all his train,
With the flag of Christ and the flag of Spain,
  Rode proudly up the bay.

In robes of scarlet and princely gold,
  On the New World's land they kneel;

In the name of Christ, whom all adore,
They christened the island San Salvador,
   For the crown of their own Castile.

And the simple islanders gazed in awe
   On the " gods from another sphere ;"
And they brought them gifts of the Yuca
     bread,
And golden trinkets, and parrots red,
   And showed them the islands near.

They told of the lords of a golden house,
   Of the mountains of Cibao,
The cavern where once the moon was born,
The hills that waken the sun at morn,
   And the isles where the spices grow.

From isle to island the ships flew on,
   Like white birds on the main,
Till the master said, "With my flags unfurled,
I have opened the gates of another world—
   I will carry the news to Spain."

It was seven months since at Palos town,
   Ere the noon of that summer's day,

The good ships sailed, with their flags un-
    furled,
In search of another and far-off world—
  And again they are in the bay.

Twelve months have passed, and the king
    again
Holds levee with all his train,
And Columbus sits at the king's right hand,
And, whether on sea or upon the land,
  Is the greatest man in Spain.

And the queen has honored him most of all—
  She has taken him by the hand :
" Don Christopher thou shalt be called
    alway ;"
And a golden cross on his heart there lay,
  And over his breast a band.

And ships she gave, and a thousand men,
  With nobles and knights in train ;
And again the convent bells they rung,
And the praise of his name was on every
    tongue,
  As he sailed for the West again—

To the hundred islands and far away
  In the heats of the torrid zone,
To gardens as fair as Hesperides,
To spice-grown forests, and scented seas
  Where no sails had ever blown;

And up and down by the New World's coast,
  And over the western main,
With but the arms of his own true word,
He lifted the flag of the blessed Lord
  And the flag of the land of Spain.

And he gave them all to the king and queen,
  And riches of things untold;
And never a ship that crossed the sea
But brought them tokens from fruit and
    tree,
  And gems from the land of gold.

Three times he had sailed to his new-found
    world,
  Five times he had crossed the main,
When, walking once by the sea, he heard,
By secret letter or secret word,
  Of a murderous plot in Spain—

How that envious persons about the court
  Had poisoned the mind of the king
By many a letter of false report,
By base suspicion of evil sort,
  And words with a traitorous sting.

And the king, half eager to hear the worst,
  For he never had been a friend,
Believed it all, and he rued the hour
He gave to the master rank and power,
  And resolved it should have an end.

So with cold pretence of the truth to hear,
  And with heart that was false as base,
A ship was hurried across the main,
With Bobadilla, false knight of Spain,
  To take the admiral's place.

O that kings should ever unkingly be!
  O that men should ever forget!
For that fatal hour the false knight came,
To the king's disgrace and the great world's
    shame,
  The star of Columbus set.

They took the queen's cross from off his
    breast,
    And chains they gave him instead;
And iron gyves on his wrists they put,
Vile fetters framed for each hand and foot—
    " 'Twere better they left him dead."

For he who was first of the new-found world,
    And bravest upon the main,
Who had found the isles of the fabled gold,
And the far-off lands that his faith foretold,
    Was dragged like a felon to Spain.

But the whole world heard the clank of his
        chains,
    When he landed in Cadiz bay;
And fearing the taunt and the curse and scoff,
The false king hurried to take them off,
    At the pier where the old ship lay.

But little it helped, or the king's false smile,
    As he sat in his robes of state;
For wrong is wrong, if in hut or hall,
And the right were as well not done at all,
    If done, alas! too late.

And little it helped if, here and there,
  The mantle of favor stole
Across his shoulders, to hide the stain
Of a broken heart or a broken chain—
  They had burned too deep in his soul.

So the years crept by, and the cold neglect
  Of kings, that will come the while;
Forever and ever 'tis still the same—
Short-lived's the glory of him whose fame
  Depends on a prince's smile.

And long he thought, could he see the queen,
  Could he speak with her face to face,
She would know the truth and would be again
What once she was, ere his hopes were slain;
  And he sighed in his lonely place.

And on a day when he seemed forgot,
  And darker the fates, and grim,
A letter came, 'twas the queen's command,
"Come straight to court," in her own fair hand,
  And she would be true to him.

But alas for man, and alas for queen,
  And alas for hopes so sped!

He had only come to the castle gate,
When the warder said, "It is late—too late,
  For the queen, she is lying dead."

And the king forgot what the fair, good queen
  With her dying lips had said;
And he who had given a world to Spain
Had never a roof for himself again,
  And he wished that he, too, were dead.

Slow tolled the bells of old Seville town,
  At noon of a summer's day;
For up in a chamber of yonder inn,
Close by the street, with its noise and din,
  The heart of the New World lay.

Perhaps the king, on his throne close by,
  No thought to the tolling gave;
But over a world, far up and down,
They heard the bells of Seville town,
  And they stood by an open grave.

And the Seville bells, they are ringing still,
  Through the centuries far and dim;
And though it is but the common lot
Of men to die, and to be forgot,
  They will ring forever of him.

THE FIRST KISS.

Can you tell me what a kiss is,
      Lady mine ?
Stands there writ among the pages
Of the poets and the sages
      Any sign ?

What a kiss is, sweet, then listen
      Once to me :
When the fairies first made lovers,
Such as you and I and others—
      In their glee,

They forgot to make a sign-word
      And a seal—
Something that should be a token
Of a something still unspoken,
      That we feel.

Till one day a man and maiden,
      Sweet as morn,
Touched their lips just so, together,
And out there, among the heather,
      It was born.

Oh! the fairies laughed and cried so,
　　In the morn,
Just to think, in two lips meeting,
And in two eyes fondly greeting,
　　It was born.

And they laughed, and said together,
　　We will make
Out of human lips a treasure,
Loved and deep beyond all measure,
　　For their sake.

And with fairy wands they touched them,
　　And the thrill
Of the two first lips together,
On that sweet morn in the heather,
　　Liveth still.

And from that morn unto this morn
　　Of our bliss,
There hath never been a lover
But the sign-word could discover
　　In a kiss.

PHILIP.

Ah! many and many a year ago it was —
And yet, but yesterday it might have been,
So little changed are fields and olive rows,
And Prato's hills, and orchards gold and
    green,
And hearts of men and women too, I ween.
Some things there are that never do grow old,
Or, growing old, age is not felt nor seen;
As faces of the ones we love — they hold
A truce with time, — and lovers' tales, though
    oft retold.

Ah! many a year within a cloister's walls,
A friar-painter brooded all the day;
For even prayer sometimes a little palls
On honest hearts who count their beads alway,
And most with those who work, as well as
    pray.
And so with Philip, young and fair, and one
Whom cities honored; and men loved to say

44

That Friar Philip painted Christ as none
In all his far-famed Italy had ever done.

Still was he not content, for he would trace
The Holy Virgin, with a face so fair,
Men should not say, " How sweet it is, what
    grace,
What depth of color and what beauty rare,
And still, no face of any *woman* there."
He would have flesh, and human blood and
    bone;
Christ was a woman's son, the priests declare:
It was a maid, on whom the starlight shone
That night, that sweetest night, God's world
    has ever known.

" If I could find in all fair Italy,
One face to help me to my face divine,
It should be riches, joy enough, for me,
Alas! there is not any face so fine
As this I see, this virgin face of mine.
If Heaven were gracious — no — it cannot
    be,
That which my soul for ever doth enshrine,

Which even in sleep comes tenderly to me,
I cannot paint because no form or body can I
    see."

One day, blessed day, within St. Margaret,
A sisters' cloister of old Prato town,
The pious abbess thought to pay some debt
To some dead saint or other, of renown,
And prayed that Philip might himself come
    down
And paint a virgin, with a mother's face,
And Christ, the child, her glory and her crown,
A picture fitted for such holy place, —
Thus would the sisters find some special last-
    ing grace.

Long up and down the archèd room he went,
With folded hands, and eyes bent down alway;
His unused easel on the altar leant,
The unstained pallet on the marble lay,
His thoughts, with her, had wandered far
    away.
"Cursed fate" — he cried — "but, no, I do
    forget —

I will not curse, and yet I cannot pray."
Thus murmured ever till his dark eyes met
The nearing, list'ning abbess of St. Margaret.

" What is it, Philip ? list — I heard you here ;
He is more gracious than your words allow —
The sweetest face of Italy is near,
I hear her singing in the vespers now —
A month ago, she took our novice vow.
It is not seeming, and perhaps not meant,
And holy fathers they would frown, I trow,
To see a novice to a brother lent,
E'en were 't to paint a picture of the sacra-
      ment.

" But you I know and your good heart ah, well,
Take her till prayers, and paint her as you
      can,
Above that altar, that we long may tell
We have a picture by the famous man ;
It is not every convent here in Prato can.
Bar well the door, and let the censer swing,
It adds a glamour to this room — a spell,
Perhaps 't will aid in your imagining,
It is like her, so fair, so beautiful a thing."

Herself she crossed, and left him at the noon—
The great drops stand in **Philip's** dark, deep
      eyes;
It is too much to be so blest so soon,
But he who falters at this moment, dies.
He laughs anon, and then anon he **sighs.**
The curtains part—along the altar stair
A rustling gown, to where his pallet lies—
His prayed-for virgin—see, she waits him
      there.
Even in his dreams she was not half so fair.

Abashed, and blushing like a rose she stood,
Her dark eyes resting on the marble floor;
"Was this not Philip, whom the sisterhood
Had praised a thousand, thousand times,
      before,
Till she herself was ready to adore?"
He took her hand and gently led to where
The sunbeams bent, embracing, from a stained
      door,
Casting their shadows on an oaken chair,
High-backed and carvèd, that was standing
      there.

High-backed and carvèd and of form antique,
And half way covered with a cloth of gold,
So bright, the very sunbeams even seemed
　　to seek
Some new warmth lurking in its secret fold —
As if when *she* were there, even marble could
　　be cold —
She was herself so warm, and beautiful, and
　　rare, —
Not half her beauty had the abbess told.
Heaven! 'tis no wonder Philip can but
　　stare,
How could mere mortal paint a face so fair?

Her novice kerchief she has laid aside,
And loosed the girdle from her simple gown,
And her sweet bodice she has half untied,
And half the abandon of her hair is down,
Her hair, so soft, and beautiful, and brown.
He looked and sighed as in a soothèd bliss,
Saw his ideal — of all maids, the crown,
The throat, the bosom, fit for cherub's kiss,
Alas! he was not living who could paint like
　　this.

He was not living who could paint a sigh,
Or the soft heaving of a loving breast,
Nor the warm lustre of a woman's eye
When he she loves is ling'ring to be prest —
Could one so paint, he were divinely blest.
He tried and tried, then laid the pallet
    down, —
The chapel bells were calling her to prayer,
Her beads she took, and, folding her sweet
    gown,
She left him longing like a spirit there,
In sad, yet sweet and beautiful despair.

But on that night, when olive-covered hills
Lay sweet and silvered with a summer moon,
When all was silence, save the whippoorwills
Who tired not chanting in the sad old roon
To the grim watchdog that had waked too
    soon,
Soft whisp'ring lips half touched a maiden's
    ear :
"Arise, arise, it is the long night's noon,
And here are kisses for thee, sweet, and here."
And softly rose she without shame or fear.

And softly stepped she on the oaken stair,
And softly stepped she in that chapel old,
The silver censer still was swinging there,
As if a moonbeam did its weight uphold,
It was so light, and beautiful of mould.
It was not mockery that she did kneel,
Though round her waist she felt an arm
enfold,
Beneath that censer it was good to feel
The old time blessing guilt could not conceal.

And out through fields, and olive groves
they went,
Through cypress alleys, and by forests green,
And purpled vines, with luscious fruits all
bent,
And high stone walls, with narrow lanes
between, —
And over all the moonlight's mellow sheen.
Still on they wandered till the coming day
Changed into purple the enchanted scene;
And when the sisters met that morn, to
pray,
They did not dream how far she was away.

Oh woe! oh woe! the sisters cried that
    morn,
And woe! swift neighbors, as they mounted
    steed;
And all the hills re-echo to the horn,
And horses' hoofs, as quickly on they speed
By brook, and bridge, and olive grove and
    mead.
In vain, in vain, not one of them may tell
Where he hath hid her in this hour of need,
If in some cave of mountain, or some secret
    dell —
Little, but little, recks he, that they ride so
    well.

Vain was demand, and vain was bishop's
    frown,
Vain as swift mounting, and the swifter
    chase —
But once, when Philip came to Prato town,
Men saw him painting, in the market-place,
The immortal picture of his lady's face —
A face so fair — a sorrow without pain,
An angel's look, and yet a woman's grace —

As if a rose upon a frost had lain,
And blushed to see itself a rose again.

Long dead is he who painted there that day,
And she whose face did so his soul inspire,
And all those sisters, aye, long dead are they;
And other hands now light that altar-fire,
And that sweet censer's like a broken lyre.
But through the ages, still men love to trace
An art new born to Philip, king and sire,
And lives like song the beauty of that face
That Philip Lippi painted in the market-place.

MARGERY BROWN.

Margery Brown is ever so fair,
 There is none like her, not one in the town.
Brown are her soft eyes, and browner her hair,
Queenly her footstep, and queenly her air—
 No, there's no other like Margery Brown.

Margery Brown is not young as she seems,
 Fair as she is from her foot to her crown,
Lips archly bent, cheeks with dimples and
  gleams,
Eyes full of summer and beautiful dreams—
 She is just sixty—sweet Margery Brown.

Years ago, many, sweet Margery Brown
 Loved as a woman can only know how;
That was the year of the plague in the town,
And people all wondered that Margery
  Brown
Kept her sweet dimples and beautiful brow.

"I am still beautiful," Margery said,
 Bowing her face to the form they laid down.

"He will come back when the poppies are red.
See! how he smiles, tho' he's lying there dead;"
  And the neighbors all pitied mad Margery
    Brown.

Years did not reckon with Margery more ;
  Time brought no dimness to eyes that
    were brown—
Fountains of youth kept her beauty in store.
" I am yet young," she still said, "as before,"
  And fair as an angel was Margery Brown.

Margery lives in a world of her own.
  What to her if the sun goes down ?
Night hath stars that never have shone,
And she has hopes none other has known.
  And they keep her young, sweet Margery
    Brown.

She forgets that the years pass by,
  Margery fair, with the quaint-cut gown,
Lips of roses and sunlit eye,
Cheeks where blushes and dimples vie ;
  But all hearts love her—sweet Margery
    Brown.

NEWS AT THE WHITE HOUSE.

ALL the night the President sat,
  Waiting the telegraph's click, click, click ;
Waiting the news that should tell him that
  Grant had crossed at the little creek ;
Waiting to hear that before the light
  Sherman's troops were beyond the bridge;
That over the river, from left to right,
  All was ready to charge the Ridge.

Chickamauga was lost; our dead
  Lay in heaps on the sodden plain ;
What if the rebel, with lifted head,
  Strike, as he struck, to our hearts again !
Over the North, as a pall of night,
  Sorrow hung, and the summons came :
" Win a victory—win us a fight ;
  Wipe away from our flag the shame."

All the night, in his room alone—
  All the night till the dawn was by,

And over the broad Potomac shone
  Red the sun in the eastern sky—
Watched the President, grave and sad—
  Came no tick on the mystic line ;
What if the daring rebel had
  Tapped the wire and read the sign—

Sign of battle, or sign of gloom?
  Hark ! the lightning's messenger !
No ! Silence only is in the room—
  Silence only, and breath of prayer.
Listen ! Yes, 'tis the tick, tick, tick—
  " Clear the lines " are the first words sent,
" Up to Washington, men, be quick !
  Grant will talk with the President."

Click, click, click, went the instrument—
  "Sherman's army has crossed the stream;"
Nearer the table the grave face leant,
  Lips half parted and eyes agleam.
" Hooker's soldiers but yesterday
  Stormed up Lookout in mist and rain ;
They are holding the dangerous way,
  They will fight at our right again.

"On the left is our storming line,
  Sherman's legions are bending on ;"
Click, click, click: " On the Ridge there shine
  Rows of cannon since early dawn—
Rows of cannon and men in gray,
  Shining columns of burnished steel ;
They are holding our men at bay,
  They are waiting the cannon's peal.

"Look ! our soldiers have climbed the Ridge;
  Sherman's gallants have stormed the line
Forty cannon are at the bridge—
  Brave these soldiers of his and mine !"
Click, click, click : " The centre moves,
  Thomas, Sheridan, all abreast,
Bayonets fixed—in troops and droves
  Charging clear to the mountain's crest.

"Battle's thunder from left to right,
  Belching cannon and musket's crash."
Click, click, click : " Lo ! on every height
  Flames of sulphur and lightnings flash."
Closer still to the breathing wire
  Bends the face of the President—

Does he hear it, the battle's fire,
  Half-way over a continent?

Does he hear it, the bugle's call,
  Sounding "Forward," the whole long line?
Sees he blue-coat and gray-coat fall?
  Hears he cannon and splintering pine?
Click, click, click : "And a thousand men
  Climb the works on the highest hill—
Wait! they are driving us back again!
  No! our banner is waving still!

"See! we're storming the whole long line,
  Waiting never a leader's cry;
Over the rocks and splintering pine—
  We will capture the Ridge or die!
Hand to hand on the very crest "—
  Click, click, click—"with the naked steel;
Only a moment, and, east to west,
  Flags are falling and columns reel.

"Shouts and cheers on the Ridge are heard—
  Shouts and cheers till the skies are rent;
Back to the river, they've got the word—
  Won is the battle, our President!"

Quick as thought, and the answer flies—
    "Bless our soldiers ! God bless each one !"
And up to the loyal Northern skies
    Hymns ascend for the battle won.

Kind, good President—brave, strong men,
    Sounds of battle you'll hear no more—
Calls of bugle to charge again,
    Crash of muskets or cannon's roar.
But, while Mountain and Ridge shall stand,
    They are one with your deathless fame ;
Men shall tell to a rescued land
    How the news to the White House came.

THE REVEILLE.

FOR the one last reveille
   They are waiting as they fell—
Arm to arm, and knee to knee ;
   They are sleeping—it is well—
Till the one last reveille.

They are sleeping—let them rest—
   In the sod they died to save ;
Fame shall write above their breast,
   "They are mine, though in the grave,"
And their spirits shall have rest.

Feet of loved ones shall come near
   When the May is in her bloom,
And with garlands every year
   Deck their unforgotten tomb,
For, though dead, they are so dear.

When, with fife and muffled drum,
   And with steady step, and slow,

They shall hear their comrades come,
 They will hear the step and know—
They will hear them when they come.

They will smell the fragrance sweet
 Of the blossoms that you bring;
They will hear the treading feet;
 They will hear the songs you sing;
They will hear the drummers beat.

They will hear the jubilee,
 And the bells that ring release—
They will fold their arms and be
 All at rest in hope and peace,
While they wait the reveille.

SAID A SONG-BIRD.

SAID a song-bird cnce to me,
  "Listen to my roundelay;
Man nor maid shall hinder me—
  I shall sing my song to-day."

Said a song-bird once to me,
  "I have sung my song to-day;
Hadst thou listened, it may be
  I have said what thou wouldst say."

I have only said and sung
  Things that in thy heart have dwelt;
Though thy harp was never strung,
  Thou hast felt what I have felt.

All are poets in their time—
  God's whole world is harmony:
Lo! in one majestic rhyme
  Sweep the rivers to the sea.

All are poets when they feel
　　Nature's rhythms rise and fall ;
Nature's heart-beats are the seal
　　Maketh poets of us all.

If, perchance, these songs of mine
　　Waken some responsive strain,
Silent though the countersign,
　　I shall not have sung in vain.

THE GUARD ON THE VOLGA.

WHAT is it you 're watching, good soldier,
  In the forest so dark and lone?
I have heard of no Turkish cannon,
  And our Czar is at peace at home.
Why stand on the Volga River,
  When the night is so cold and drear?
My Christ! must a soldier shiver,
  When never a foeman is near?

Hark! peasant, across there, an army
  Lies hid in the brushwood and moss,
And the sergeant said: " Watch by the ferry,
  And see that no picket shall cross."
I charged the red ditches at Plevna,
  And knew the foes' sabres by sight.
It was fierce! it was death! but I never
  Knew fear in my life till to-night.

By Heavens! I tremble. What is it?
  What is it, this army so near?

Why don't the drums beat to the rescue?
　　Why is not our Skobeleff here?
Are hordes of the desert upon us,
　　Are China's fierce legions at war,
And we but one guard on the Volga?
　　God save our good land and the Czar!

A fiercer foe, far, than the Tartar, —
　　And armies of China are small
When counted beside the battalions
　　That muster to conquer them all.
'T is the Pestilence marching in silence,
　　That hides in the brushwood and moss;
But the sergeant said: "Stick to the ferry,
　　And see that no picket shall cross."

Great God!   Do they think that a picket
　　Can stop what the Heavens command?
That bullets may wrestle with angels,
　　To keep the Plague out of the land?
Oh! soldier, I 'm but a poor peasant,
　　Yet know that God has but one way.
Trust sabre, nor rifle, nor picket,
　　But kneel by the Volga and pray.

And peasant and soldier together
    Knelt down in the forest alone,
And prayed that that night on the Volga
    The hand of the Lord should be shown.
And though the Plague lurks on the border,
    And hides 'mid the brushwood and moss,
God's angels keep watch o'er the ferry,
    And see that no picket shall cross.

THE SEA.

A CHARM there is about the dang'rous sea
That draws man to its rugged arms, as draws
The polar star the compass to the North.
Let him but taste the briny ocean once, —
Friends, home, nor gold, can stay his wild
    desire
To breast again its waves, to breathe its air,
To brave its tempests, and to share its calm.
To him, the deep, with all its heartless wreck
And ruin, is a thing to love. Its storms
Are playthings to his daring heart. He
    sleeps
Amid its foaming rage, as sleeps a child
Upon some mossy bank, nor dreams of harm
To happen, ere his day has come.
                         To be
Upon its billowy breast, sweetheart and wife,
Mother and child, are left to weep and wait
Through weary days, weeks, months, and
    years ; and when

At last the longed-for sailor comes, 't is but
To snatch one kiss of love, a wife's embrace,
A mother's tear — then yield himself again
To that strange spell which binds him to the
    sea.
Again he tramps the vessel's deck; climbs
    high
Among its shrouds and sails, and feels again
The white sea-foam leap up to greet him with
Its rude embrace. His heart is strangely full,
And all he has he gives to his best love,
The sea — his youth, his manhood, and at last
Himself; then sweetly sleeps the long strange
    sleep
Of Death in the old Ocean's arms.

AUF WIEDERSEHEN!

There are no words in our cold English
    tongue
Where hope and joy are kin alike to pain;
"Farewell," we say, and the sad heart is
    wrung:
    Only farewell—there is no " wiedersehen;"

No wish expressed, no joyous hope, that
    when,—
    The voyage ended o'er the dang'rous main,
The desert crossed, the trial done,—that then
    We, who have parted thus, may meet again.

Not so farewell the German sailor cries,
    Not so good-by, sad sweetheart unto swain.
I go to come—he is not dead who dies;
    Good-by, sweet love,—but, till we meet
    again.

"Auf wiedersehen"—a hundred thoughts in
   one—
The double joy that recompenses pain:
There is a rising as a setting sun;
   Good-by, sweet love, good-by—"auf wie-
   dersehen."

"Auf wiedersehen"—good-by, but not for
   aye;
Thou still shalt be my one sweet song's
   refrain.
Though thou dost go, thus ever shalt thou
   stay,—
   Good-by, sweet love, good-by—"auf wiedersehen."

"Auf wiedersehen"—good-by, good-by, and
   when
Hope hath, in trust, the wicked absence
   slain,
I will be with you every hour; till then
   Good-by, sweet love, good-by—"auf wiedersehen."

THE TRAMP OF SHERMAN'S ARMY.

List, comrades, I hear the old bugle ;
  It's sounding the same reveille
That wakened the armies of Sherman
  One morn by the swift Tennessee.
A thousand old memories crowd on me ;
  My tired feet are marching along,
Keeping steps with the notes of yon bugle,
  Or the words of some old army song.

I see Hooker's lines climbing Lookout,
  The storming of Sherman's brave men,
The "Ridge," and the Centre, and Thomas,
  The flag floating up there again ;
And Grant standing there like a statue,
  Unmoved till the battle is done ;
And the words of great Lincoln, I hear them—
  "God bless you, brave men, every one."

And the fields fiercely fought for Atlanta,
  Once more to my vision they rise—

A hundred long days, each a battle,
   And nights full of dread and surprise.
Each mountain and hill grows historic ;
   Each stream from some battle is red ;
Each field is swift mown with war's sickle ;
   Each hillock's some grave of our dead.

I see the flag float o'er Atlanta—
   The tattered old flag that we bore
At Shiloh and Vicksburg and Corinth,
   And a score of red battles before.
With a cheer on the ramparts we raise it,
   A cheer, and a sigh for our men
Who sleep in the woods over yonder,
   Who'll never see battle again.

* * * * * * *

Again the old bugle is sounding ;
   There's a tramping of thousands of men ;
The mountains repeat the wild music ;
   The forests re-echo again.
And around every camp-fire's the story
   Of fame and of glory to be,
And a shout of blue-coated battalions,
   For Sherman will march to the sea.

And look! the great columns are moving
  To music of bugle and drum ;
Their blood-colored flags pointing south-
    ward,
  Like tempests the blue columns come,
While millions stand breathlessly waiting
  The boom of a far signal-gun,
For the blaze of that cannon shall tell them
  How bravely Savannah was won.

Oh! where are the men who took Lookout,
  Or stormed up the "Ridge" on that day?
Who held the hot lines at the "Tunnel,"
  Or drove the fierce foeman to bay?
Oh! where are the legions of Sherman?   ·
  God bless them, wherever they be,
Who fought with him all that war-summer,
  Or marched with him down to the sea.

Where, where are the heroes who wakened
  That morn by the swift Tennessee,
When the bugles of Sherman said "For-
    ward,"
  Or sounded their loud reveille?

Where, where are the men of Resaca,
   Of Dallas, of Kenesaw—where?
Fame writ their names up in her temple,
   And Freedom stands guarding them there.

Oh patriots! oh comrades! we know you;
   Your hands are still touching our own;
The flag that we saved there together—
   No star from its glory has flown.
Again we touch elbows; your spirits
   Are with us to-night in this room;
There's Logan, I know by his bearing,
   McPherson I see by his plume.

There's Sheridan riding his charger,
   And Thomas, so brave and serene,
And Hooker, and Grant, the great captain,
   His eye resting still on the scene;
And spirits of blue-coated soldiers
   Are wheeling from column to line;
They see the great chief and salute him,
   And give him the new countersign.

Fill up again, comrades, your glasses;
   Let's drink to these spirits, and be

Once more the old army of Sherman,
 That stood by the blue Tennessee.
Let's keep the old camp-fires a-burning,
 The songs and the memories bright,
Till the bugle shall sound by yon river—
 All hail! and forever—good-night!

THE BALLAD OF QUINTIN MASSY.

WHO goes to the city of Antwerp, that famous old Flemish town,
Will see, in the square of the Münster, a
fountain of great renown.

It stands by the grand Cathedral, the church
with the wondrous chimes,
And the maidens go there for water, as they
went in the olden times;

And they meet and talk of their lovers, till
their pitchers are running o'er,
And wonder if Flemish lovers will be what
they were, once more, —

Will be what they were when Quintin, as
famous in art as in love,
·Wrought out from the heated iron the
Roland that stands above.

As gallant a youth was Quintin as any in
Antwerp town,

And never a better blacksmith made bellows
go up and down ;

And never a Flanders lover had maiden more
richly fair,
Than the daughter of proud Franz Floris,
renowned of the painters there.

But the haughty, the proud Franz Floris
looked up from his easel, and said :
" The world it has got but one Floris, with
only one child to wed.

And he who will woo and win her, must first
be a painter, and paint
This fairest of faces in Flanders, — knight-
errant, or king, or saint.

I note that you are a blacksmith, and a
clever one, too, they say —
There are many fair girls in Antwerp would
marry you any day.

But the daughter of old Franz Floris can
never give heart nor hand
To one who is not the equal of any in all the
land."

" Now, good Franz Floris, listen — I 'll tell ·
   you what I will do —
There is not in the whole of Flanders a
   painter so great as you ;

But if, within five short summers, I paint on
   a canvas clear,
A picture better than any of all you have
   painted here, —

Do you promise upon your honor, do you
   promise your own good name,
That she shall be mine forever ? be one in
   my love — my fame ? "

Loud laughed the great Franz Floris : " Too
   modest, young man, by far.
Art is not won like a maiden, nor maidens
   as some things are.

I grant that to be a blacksmith, to hammer
   a nail or a ring,
Is an easy task for a young man, but *art*
   is another thing.

And whether my daughter is willing to wait
   five summers for you ?

There are enough of Antwerp's gallants who
  wait but my leave to woo."

"I 'll wait!" cried Floris' daughter; "I 'll
  wait, good Quintin, nor wed;
Five summers will find me faithful, or else
  they will find me dead."

So he buckled his sword about him, and with
  pilgrim's staff in hand,
He wandered along fair rivers, he journeyed
  through many a land;

And an image was ever before him: "Could
  I paint what my soul doth see,
There is not a painter in Flanders, who would
  not be envying me."

So out from the fields of Holland, and over
  cold fields of snow,
By many an Alpine torrent, by many a gorge
  below,

The feet of the pilgrim wandered, far into
  that favored clime,
Where art is a child of nature, and nature
  a thing sublime.

Then he tarried and sought a master, in
color, and form, and line,
And watched the summer sunsets go out in
a sea of wine.

And the days went by, and the summers
in splendor their cycles ran,
And the smith became a scholar, and the
scholar the fullgrown man.

Five years to a day had vanished, five years
and a month had flown,
And the autumn had brought no message to
her who was left alone.

" He is dead," she cried, " my lover, for faith-
less he could not be ; "
" He is dead," the false winds whispered,
" he is dead, but not for thee."

One day, when the great Franz Floris stood
leaning on Quintin's well,
A pedler unloosed his bundle, with curious
things to sell :

" For the love of God, buy something ! I
have nothing to eat or wear !

I am told you are fond of pictures, and here
  I have one that's rare :

It has neither frame nor stretcher — but the
  colors remain as clear " —
" What is that ? good heaven ! " cried Floris,
  " 't is my child that is painted here.

Who — where is the master painter ? how
  much is the price you seek ?
There is not a man in Flanders can paint such
  a brow and cheek."

" Thank   God ! "   the stranger answered,
  "thank God that you think it true,
For that picture is Quintin Massy's, who
  claims your daughter of you."

"If you are Quintin Massy, and if this is
  the work of your hand,
There is not such another painter in all of
  this Flemish land.

There's not such another painter, but I 've
  news that is sad for you,
And if you are Quintin Massy, you 'll know
  what I say is true : —

Five summers my child had waited, five
summers their autumns wed,
And the winter brought no message, and the
poor child thought thee dead.

'He is dead,' she cried, 'my lover, for faith-
less he could not be;'
'He is dead,' the false winds whispered, 'he
is dead, but not for thee.'

This morning, this very morning, when the
cloister bells strike nine,
There will be another sister at the cloister
of Isoline;

When—the bell strikes nine and a quarter,
she will kneel for the one last vow,—
'Tis a mile from here, good Quintin, and the
bells are ringing now."

" Horse — horse ! " cries Quintin Massy, and
his cloak is cast afar,
And he rides with sword and buckler, as a
soldier would ride to war.

The bell strikes five already — the bell strikes
six — and eight,

But Quintin's sword has rattled the bars of
the cloister gate.

"Who comes?" cries the angered abbess,
"who storms at the cloister door?
I tell you that Floris' daughter is a child of
the world no more.

For the solemn mass is chanting, and she
kneels at the altar rail,
And pious nuns attend her, and bring her
the sisters' veil."

"Stop, stop your prayers," cries Quintin,
"for I swear by Antwerp town,
You'll bring me Floris' daughter, or I'll
burn your cloister down."

And the pale, poor nuns grew whiter, as
white as the bands they wore,
And they led a maiden fainting, and veiled,
to the cloister door.

"It is done!" cried Quintin Massy, "the
picture I saw, is done!
And as you are Floris' daughter, so I am
to be his son."

And the chimes of the famous Münster rang
  out in a joyous tune,
As the bride and her blacksmith painter rode
  by on that afternoon.

BABY HELÉNE.

She was only a child of the May-day,
   That came when the sweet blossoms fell,
But rarer than any fair lady
   Of whom the old poets may tell.
Then the days brought us everything sweeter
   Of sunshine and love in their train,
But better than all and completer,
         Was Baby Heléne.

With a kiss and a smile she came to us,
   The sunshine of God in her hair,
Ah! never a sweet wind that blew us
   A blossom so tender and rare.
We sang a new May-song together,
   New-found and of jubilant strain,
Ah! our hearts they were light as a feather,
         With Baby Heléne.

Would she stay with us, love us? We bid her
   Unloosen the notes of her song —

And tell where the sweet angels hid her,
   And why had we waited so long.
Would they sorrow in Heaven to miss her?
   Would they wait for her, weary to pain?
Would they anger to see us but kiss her,
      Our Baby Heléne?

And all the day long, like new lovers,
   Like words that are ever in tune,
Like songs the fresh May-wind discovers,
   Like birds that are mating in June, —
Together we loved and we wandered,
   Forgetting of sorrow or pain,
Forgetting the sweets that we squandered,
      With Baby Heléne.

Oh! lips running over to kisses,
   Red cheeks kissed to brown by the sun,
Shall we ever again know what bliss is,
   When the song and the kisses are done?
Oh! baby, brown-haired, on thy tresses
   The hands of the angels had lain,
And joy laughed new-born in caresses
      Of Baby Heléne.

Years went — seven years with their story
　　More bright than Aladdin's of old,
To love and be loved was our glory,
　　Our hearts were our castles of gold.
But broken our castles, and falling,
　　Hope crushed — true hearts bleeding and
　　　　slain,
God's angels in Heaven were calling
　　　　　Our Baby Heléne.

Dim-eyed, and heart-broken, we waited
　　The sounds of invisible things,
While the soul of our soul was remated,
　　Borne off on invisible wings.
In the far-away, purple and golden,
　　Went up an ineffable strain,
And the far-away gates were unfolden
　　　　　To Baby Heléne.

One moment, God's earth and its brightness
　　Seemed darkened and turned into dross,
And the manifold stars and their lightness
　　Were dimmed and as nothing to us.
For the bowl that was golden was broken,
　　The hearts that were one heart, were twain.

And the last words of love had been spoken .
By Baby Heléne.

Ah! seven years gone as the dream goes,
  Oh! baby-love, lost to our ken, —
Will the brooklet still flow where the stream
    flows?
  Will the lilies still blossom as then?
Will the sweet tongues of birds be unloosed
    to
  The songs of our love and its pain?
Will the violets bloom as they used to
    For Baby Heléne?

Oh! baby-love, heart-sweet, the sunlight
  That fell on the way that you went,
Shall be to our feet as the one light,
  The lamp the sweet angels have lent.
And the nights and the days shall be lighter,
  And the ways that were dark ways be plain,
And the stars where thou art shall be brighter
    For Baby Heléne.

THE DWARF OF MYTILENE.

THERE dwelt in Mytilene once,
　　By the Ægæan sea,
A little wrinkled, dwarfish man,
　　No uglier could there be ;
But a very prince of ferrymen,
　　And stout of limb was he.

No man had ever vainly dared,
　　No woman feared to go,
To any island in that sea,
　　Whatever winds might blow,
If only Phaon's boat were there,
　　And Phaon's self, to row.

For men have seen him when the waves
　　Grew loud and thick apace,
When wild winds blew from Asia's sides,
　　And storms came down from Thrace,
Sail out as if to dare their rage,
　　And fight them face to face.

And yet a life of woe was his,
  On land or stormy main;
No bright eyes ever on him smiled,
  No sweet voice called his name;
In sun, or shade, or storm, or calm,
  His days were all the same.

Proud maidens of the Lesbian Isle,
  Proud men of high degree,
Curled their cold lips, and passed him by,
  As one unfit to be;
And children shouted, "See, he comes,
  The old man of the sea."

One day in the sweet summer-time,
  There came across the hills
The kindly lowing of the herds,
  The songs of many rills,
And the old man leaned him on his oar,
  And thought upon his ills.

He thought of those proud Lesbian dames,
  And those proud-hearted men —
He cursed his bitterness of fate,
  He cursed the gods, and then

Wished that the sun that saw him born
  Had never shone again.

He dropped his oar, he crossed his arms,
  When o'er the sands apace
A step drew near.   He turned and saw
  A fair young woman's face —
No maiden was there like to her
  In all the Lesbian race.

"O, who art thou, thou queenly maid?
  From whence now may'st thou be?"
"I am the Queen of Love," she said:
  "Wilt bear me o'er the sea?
For yonder, on that island fair,
  Adonis waits for me."

O, never yet had ferryman
  A passenger so fair, —
O, never had the sun shone on
  So strangely matched a pair,
As wrinkled Phaon at the oars,
  And Venus smiling there.

The boat went up, the boat went down,
  Forward and forward still,

While Phaon stood behind the oars,
  And worked with mighty will.
And Mytilene's lights grew dim,
  On every tower and hill.

The land was reached, the harbor passed,
  The goddess sprang on shore.
" What shall I pay, good ferryman,
  Since thou hast brought me o'er ? "
And Phaon, bowing, answered her,
  " Thy smiles, and nothing more."

" A woman's smiles," the goddess said,
  " May come or go at will,
They slay as often as they bless,
  Nor pity when they kill.
But thou shalt have a richer fate,
  A dowry better still."

She touched the girdle at her side, —
  Transformed, the old man stood,
The fairest mortal ever seen
  On the Ægæan flood —
A dwarf, in one sweet moment made
  The equal of a god.

ECHO.

THERE was a young nymph Echo, once,
Employed by thundering Jove,
To entertain his queen at home,
Whene'er he wished to rove;
  To talk, and talk, and talk with her,
  And keep her mind away,
  Whilst he with nymphs and goddesses
  Went sporting many a day.

Thus hours and days, the legends tell,
Good Juno's king was gone,
And little did the queen suspect
What errands he was on;
  For by her side, incessantly,
  In court or pleasant walk,
  Fair Echo laughed and gave no time
  For anything but talk.

She talked poor Juno mad almost,
Until by her 't was seen

It was a ruse of Jupiter
To blind an injured queen :
    When turning on the nymph, she cried,
    " Far shall my vengeance reach, —
    Behold! false maid, from this time forth
    Thou shalt be robbed of speech."

She touched her with her wand, and lo !
The sweet nymph's tongue was fast —
Of others' words she still had voice
To echo back the last ;
    But from her own sad, swelling heart,
    No word might ever come, —
    In burning pain, or thrilling joy,
    Still were her own lips dumb.

Through field, and grove, and silent wood,
She wandered here and there,
And meeting with Narcissus once,
She loved the stripling fair.
    But what is love unspoken worth,
    Or lips to silence wed ? —
    Though she was young, and fair as
        young,
    Narcissus saw and fled.

Grieving, she wept, and turned her face, —
She heard the ring-dove moan,
Oh! pity, pity, pity love
Forsaken by its own.
    And up and down, and far and wide,
    She walked, and sadly wept,
    And she was like some lily fair
    Whereon the frost had slept.

Oh! never, never such a maid
In the wide world was seen,
As Echo, sorrowing up and down,
By wood and meadow green;
    And her fair body pined, and grew
    Like to the air, so thin —
    The sunshine found no cheek to kiss,
    No heart to enter in.

Like to the mem'ry of a dream
She grew, and faded, till
Nought but her echoing voice was left,
To gladden wood and hill;
    And half ashamed, and half afraid,
    Like to some naiad queen

She hid herself among the rocks,
And nevermore was seen.

The wild birds sought her on the hill,
The huntsman on the plain --
She laughed, and mocked, and cried, but still
Was never seen again, —
    But summer evenings, schoolboys hear,
    In woods and valleys fair,
    The nymph, whom Juno's vengeance
      turned
    Into an echo there.

THE KISS OF JUPITER.

In ages past, when Jupiter
  Was wandering here and there,
He peeping in a temple saw
  Sweet Io bent in prayer,
And quite forgetful of his wife,
  He kissed the maiden fair.

A rousing kiss it must have been,
  Resounding far and near,
For Juno on Olympus heard,
  And hurrying through the air,
Threw wide the temple doors and stood
  Before the guilty pair.

One look on Jupiter she cast,
  One on the maid, — and lo!
She turned her with her wand into
  A heifer white as snow —
With Argus, hundred-eyed, to watch
  Wherever she might go.

And up and down, and far and wide,
  Go where the poor cow will,
That cursèd herdsman follows her
  By field, and wood, and hill :
By day, by night, his hundred eyes
  Are burning on her still.

One day, in pity, Jupiter
  Bade Mercury repair
And find the herdsman in the woods,
  Who kept the heifer fair,
And, though he had a thousand eyes,
  To slay him then and there.

With flute and lyre flies the god
  Through woods and tangled ways —
The herdsman sees him by the brook
  And listens while he plays ;
For every song the sweet boy sings
  Is in the herdman's praise.

Enchanted music fills his ear :
  By flattery's strains misled,
He sleeps upon the dewy grass,
  Nor cunning foe doth dread, —

The god beholds the drooping eyes,
  And strikes the herdsman dead.

Rejoiced, the heifer sprang away,
  Released from Argus' eye,
And hoped in wider fields to range,
  And greener grass to try —
But lo ! beside her, day and night,
  There buzzed a mighty fly.

Enraged, the wife of Jupiter
  Had seen her herdsman slain,
And sent the gad-fly to the cow,
  To sting her into pain,
And bade it ever follow her,
  Through wood, and field, and plain.

Through many fields the poor cow ran,
  Through weary forests wide,
O'er many straggling brooks she leaped,
  And plunged through many a tide ;
Yet was that cursèd dragon-fly
  Still buzzing at her side.

It followed her through Macedon,
  It followed her through Thrace ;

It buzzed in many distant lands ;
    It stung in many a place ;
And north or south, or east or west,
    That fly was on the chase.

She swam the bounding Bosporus,
    It stung and buzzed the while,
On right and left, behind and front,
    For many a weary mile,
Till, wretched with the horrid race,
    She plunged into the Nile.

While struggling with the flood, behold !
    Eternal Jove was there,
And with his wand transformed his love,
    Into a maiden fair ;
The same whom he had kissed one morn.
    In temple nave at prayer.

And lo ! a king was waiting her.
    By Jupiter's command,
He sprang into the flood and took
    The sweet maid by the hand,
And made her mistress of his heart
    And queen of all the land.

And ever, when the new moon rose,
  It was a fancy there,
The snow-white cow's two horns were seen,
  And Io, young and fair ;
And maidens loved to hear how Jove
  Once kissed her, when at prayer.

ON A FAIR DEAD GIRL.

How beautiful to die as does the rose,
Sweet fragrance casting on the am'rous air !
What if too lovely seemed life's way to close,
When death still leaves us with a scene so
    fair.

Like to the rose thy life was one sweet
    bloom,
Till Fate undid thee from the fair young
    stem ;
It is not fit, this silent pall and plume,
These weeping maidens, and these sorrowing
    men.

Thou hadst fair youth, and life's sweet things
    the best,
Knew naught of Sorrow, or its lonely consort
    Pain ;
Thou hadst the joys of life — leave us the
    rest,
Who well have known how much of life is
    vain.

Thy cup, half finished, flushed with joyous
    wine,
The sad dregs at its bottom thou didst never
    reach ;
Thy night of revels had no morn's repine,
No aching heart, no long-regretted speech.

Thou didst not live the ignomy to own
Of beauty faded, or of roses fled ;
Thy cheeks, they paled not, ere the buds
    were blown,
Thou wert not fairer when thou lived, than
    dead.

Death is no victor thus — we will not weep !
Thou walk'st in other paths of beauty now,
    more strange ;
It is not Death we call this thing, but Sleep ;
No parting this, but Beauty's secret change.

MY WHITE ROSE AND RED.

So you've come from the South, have you,
  darlings?
  And slept snug as mice all the way?
And wasn't it cold on the mountains,
  For rosebud, and myrtle, and bay?
And *she* packed you up so together,
  And blessed you, and kissed you, and said,
" Keep sweet as my memory for him is,
  My darlings, my white rose and red."
And what did she tell you at parting?
  Some message for me, I know well;
Some praise of our boy, there, God bless him!
  Some words of our sweet little Nell.
And the dear tiny hands of the children,
  Have they touched your petals so fair?
O, rosebuds, you're happy if Helen
  But kissed you one moment, when there!
This white rose shall bloom in the study,
  This red one I'll wear on my breast,

O, I wonder if she will be thinking
  How often your petals are pressed?
Did she tell you how long we've been
    married?
  Ten years — 't is another year, soon, —
And though we've had snow in December,
  We've always had roses in June.
How far it is here from San Remo,
  The gem of the beautiful sea!
But you've come with your petals all fra-
    grant
  With incense, from her unto me.
How strange it all is; and her letter —
  This much and this only it said :
" The children are well here, and happy,
  And my love's like the white rose and
    red."
I'll write her no letter to-morrow,
  But something I'll send her instead —
Two rose leaves, — she'll guess at their
    meaning,
  One each from the white rose and red.

THE MARRIAGE OF THE FLOWERS.

"It is six," the swallows twittered, "and
    you're very late in rising,
  If you really think of rising on this lovely
    morn at all;
For the great red sun is peeping over wood
    and hill and meadow,
  And the unmilked cows are lowing in the
    dimly lighted stall."

O, ye robins and ye swallows, thought I,
    throwing back the lattice,
  Ye are noisy, joyous fellows, and you
    waken when you will;
Then I saw a dainty letter, bound in ribbon-
    grass and clover,
  That the swallows had left swinging by
    the narrow window-sill.

O, the dainty, dainty letter, on an orange
    leaf, or lemon,
  Signed, " Your friend, the Queen of Roses,"
    writ in characters of dew,
" You 're invited to the garden, there 's a good
    time there at seven,
  And a place beside the apple-tree has been
    reserved for you.

" There 'll be matings there, and marriages,
    of every flower and blossom :
  Cross the brook behind the arbor, and
    come early, if you can."
O, my thoughts, they all went bounding,
    and my heart leaped in my bosom,
  " And how sweetly she composes," I re-
    flected as I ran.

There she sat, the Queen of Roses, with her
    virgins all about her,
  While the lilacs and the apple-blooms
    seemed waiting her command.
O how lovely, O how gracious, she did smile
    on each new-comer !
  O how sweet she kissed the lilies as she
    took them by the hand !

Never had I seen her fairer than she was this
 happy morning,
 Never knew her breath delicious, half so
 boundless, half so rare;
Oh! she seemed a thing of heaven, with the
 dew upon her bosom,
 And I wished I were some daffodil, that I
 might kiss it there.

All at once the grass rows parted, and the
 sweetest notes were sounded, —
 There was music, there was odor, there was
 loving, in the air;
And a hundred joyous gallants, robed in
 holiday apparel,
 Danced beneath the lilac-bushes with a
 hundred maidens fair.

There were tulips, proud and yellow, with
 their great green spears beside them;
 There were lilies grandly bowing to the
 Rose Queen as they came;
There were daffodils so stately, scenting all
 the air of heaven,
 Joyous buds, and sleepy poppies, with
 their banners all aflame.

There were pansies robed in purple, marching
    o'er the apple-blossoms,
    And the foxgloves with their pages tripped
      coquettishly along;
And the violets and the daisies, in their
    bonnets blue and yellow,
    Joined the marching and parading of th'
      innumerable throng.

All at once the dandelion blew three notes
    upon his trumpet:
    "Choose ye partners for the dancing, gal-
      lant knights and ladies fair!"
And the honeysuckle curtsied to the young
    sweet-breathed clematis,
    And remarked upon the sweetness of the
      blossoms in her hair.

"We 're the tallest," said the tuberose to the
    iris standing nearest,
    "And suppose that now, for instance, I
      should offer you my heart?"
"O, how sudden!" cried the sly thing;
    "I 'm really quite embarrassed, —
    Unexpected, but pray do it, just to give
      the rest a start."

Then a daisy kissed a pansy, with its jacket
brown and yellow,
And a crocus led a thistle to a seat beside
the rose;
And the Maybells grouped together, close
beside the lady-slipper,
And commented on her beauty, and the
splendor of her clothes.

"O, a market this for beauty!" said a
jasmine, gently clinging
To the strong arm of an orange, as a glance
on him she threw;
"Why, you scarcely would believe it, but
I've had this very morning
Twenty offers, and declined them just to
promenade with you."

So, in groupings, or in couples, led each
knight some gentle lady,
Led some fair companion blushing, past
the windows fresh and green,
And the Sweet Rose gave her blessing, and
a kiss at times, it may be,
To the fairest brides and sweetest mortals
eye hath ever seen.

Then again the grass it parted, and the
    sunshine it grew brighter,
      Till it seemed as if the curtains of high
      heaven were withdrawn,
And each flower and bud and blossom pressed
    some fair one to its bosom,
      As the bannered train danced gayly 'twixt
      the windows on the lawn.

O, the muskrose was so stately! and so
    stately was the Queen Rose!
      And how sweetly smiled she on me, as she
      whispered in my ear:
"Come again! you know you're welcome!
    come again, dear, for, it may be
      That our baby buds and blossoms will be
      christened here next year."

ROOM FOR THE ANGELS.

FAR away by the Indus River,
Where the mornings are gold and red,
The mourners walk together,
And bury their silent dead,
In couples and in silence,—
But ever a place ahead
Is left unfilled and honored,
As that where the angels tread.

'T is a fancy, old as their river,
That, whenever they bury their dead,
The noise of wings is near them,
And light forms marching ahead,—
So ever before the mourners,
And close to the pall and plume,
'T is a beautiful heathen custom
To make for the angels room.

I've thought if some, not heathen,
Would make, in their worldly care,
Just room in their hearts for angels,
They would sometimes find them there.
If but in some nook or corner,
Filled up with the smallest things,
'T were a joy to be sometimes hearing
The rustle of angels' wings.

IF YOU WANT A KISS, WHY, TAKE IT.

THERE 's a jolly Saxon proverb,
    That is pretty much like this —
A man is half in heaven,
    When he has a woman's kiss.
But there 's danger in delaying,
    And the sweetness may forsake it;
So I tell you, bashful lover,
    If you want a kiss, why, take it.

Never let another fellow
    Steal a march on you in this,
Never let a laughing maiden
    See you spoiling for a kiss:
There 's a royal way to kissing,
    And the jolly ones who make it,
Have a motto that is winning —
    If you want a kiss, why, take it.

Any fool may face a cannon,
    Any booby wear a crown;

But a man must win a woman,
    If he 'd have her for his own. —
Would you have the golden apple,
    You must find the tree and shake it;
If the thing is worth the having,
    And you want a kiss, why, take it.

Who would burn upon a desert,
    With a forest smiling by?
Who would give his sunny summer
    For a bleak and wintry sky?
O, I tell you there 's a magic,
    And you cannot, cannot break it,
For the sweetest part of loving
    Is to want a kiss and take it.

THE MOWING.

THE clock has struck six,
And the morning is fair,
While the east in red splendor is glowing;
There is dew on the grass, and a song in the air,
Let us up and be off to the mowing.

Wouldst know why I wait,
Ere the sunlight has crept
O'er the fields where the daisies are growing?
Why all night I 've kept my own vigils, nor
slept?
'T is to-day is the day of the mowing.

This day and this hour
Maud has promised to tell
What the blush on her cheek was half show-
ing, —
If she wait at the lane, I 'm to know all is
well,
And there 'll be a good time at the
mowing.

117

Maud's mother has said,

And I'll never deny,

That a girl's heart there can be no knowing —

Oh! I care not to live, and I rather would
die,

If Maud does not come to the mowing.

What is it I see?

'Tis a sheen of brown hair,

In the lane where the poppies are blowing.

Thank God! it is Maud — she is waiting me
there,

And there'll be a good time at the
mowing.

Six years have passed by,

And I freely declare

That I scarcely have noticed their going;

Sweet Maud is my wife, with her sheen of
brown hair —

And we had a good time at the mowing.

JAMIE 'S COMING O'ER THE MOOR.

JAMIE 's coming o'er the moor,
  Heaven smile, and good betide him!
I am rich and Jamie 's poor,
  But I love no one beside him.

Jamie, Jamie, all the day, —
  I am thinking only of him ;
June would not be June alway,
  If I did not see and love him.

Twelve sweet months ago we met.
  Twelve sweet moons have been the token,
Break, my heart, or else forget
  Jamie yet no word hath spoken.

List ! 't is Jamie's voice I hear,
  One sweet voice of all the many.
I shall have no longer fear, —
  Jamie cries, " I love you, Jeannie ! "

Jamie comes across the moor,
   Heaven smile, and love betide him;
Neither I nor Jamie 's poor,
   When I love no one beside him.

MAID AND BUTTERFLY.

(From the German.)

A MAIDEN idly wandered
   Through wood and cool retreat,
And as she stopped to gather
   A nosegay from the heather,
A butterfly passed by her,
   And kissed her lips so sweet.

"O! pardon," said the rover,
   "O! pardon, maiden fair,
I sought amid the flowers
   The honey that is ours,
And took your red lips blooming
   For roses growing there."

"For this time said the maiden,
   Forgiveness — it is by ;
But I must beg to mention,
   And press to your attention,
These roses are not blooming,
   For *every* butterfly."

O, HOW SHALL I SING TO MY
FAIR ONE?

O, how shall I sing to my fair one?
  O, how tune my harp to the best?
Sweet south-winds, ye breathed on the rarest;
  Ye knew not your treasure, O West,
Wake, wake, ye red roses, half sleeping —
  Know ye that a fairer is there?
O primroses, primroses weeping!
  Hast seen her — my own one, so fair?

O morning, rejoice in my gladness!
  And breathe on my song but a tone:
She will hear — she will hear it — and answer,
  And think the sweet music my own.
O sunlight, that gladdens the hillside,
  O rainbows, that die in the sea —
Thou lendest the robes of thy beauty,
  But think not thou 'rt fairer than she.

O seas! be ye glad in my gladness!
　And hills, let me never in vain
Call out to thy heart for an echo,
　Some sound that resembles her name.
Stars brightly shine, bright on my treasure,
　˘And tell what ye dare not conceal —
O winds, help my harp to some measure,
　To words that shall speak what I feel.

UNDER THE ROSE.

SHE is not dead we love,
   She still is here ;
Cross her white hands above
   Heart true and dear.
With her new senses born,
   All things are fair ;
Brighter the stars at morn,
   Sweeter the air.

Bloom, rose, yellow rose,
   White rose, for her ;
Scent every air that blows,
   Sweet balm and fir.
Song-birds, singing still,
   Sing the old song ;
Thrush, lark, and whippoorwill,
   Sweet notes prolong.

Shine, mornings, sweet and fair—
   Shine as ye shone ;

She breathes your scented air,
  Though she be gone.
She sees the roses born
  With her new eyes;
She sees the light of morn
  Burst in the skies.

Speak, friends, in love of her—
  Speak, she is near;
What though no cloud may stir?
  Still she will hear;
Speak as ye spake before,
  Kindly and true;
There's but an open door
  'Twixt her and you.

What though her body rest
  Under the sod?
He knoweth what is best—
  Trust her to God.
Under the roses there,
  White rose and red,
She breathes the sweeter air;
  She is not dead.

She is not dead we love,
　She still is here ;
Cross her white hands above
　Heart true and dear.
Pray, friends, that when for you
　Life, too, shall close,
You seem as kind and true,
　Under the rose.

O MAIDEN, SO SLENDER AND FAIR.

O MAIDEN, so slender and fair,
  And straight as the reeds by the sea :
The rose in thy beautiful hair
  Is more than a rose unto me.

Last night, when the stars were aglow,
  We walked on the terrace, and then
You whispered this night I should know
  If I were most blessèd of men.

How queenly you look, and how rare !
  My heart is ill-trained, and I can
But look at that rose in your hair,
  And curse every daughter of man.

Walk down the bright aisles of the hall,
  So tall and so stately, — perchance
Your eyes may not meet mine at all,
  But I shall see you in the dance.

And if, when he touches your hand,
  My dagger shall leap from my side,
Ah! better the rage of the damned
  Than the wrath of a lover denied.

Oh! never you dreamed I was near,
  To-day, when you met at the train —
'T was little, I grant, I could hear,
  But that little's undoing my brain.

I saw him reach over and break
  This very same rose that you wear, —
" To-night, at the ball, for my sake,"
  Were the words that he uttered, I swear.

What? waited to see would he kiss
  The lips I had dreamed would be mine, —
Enough! there is murder in this!
  And the rose in your hair is the sign.

Yes, maiden, walk down the bright aisle,
  'T is gay here and light as the moon,
His eyes will keep time with your smile,
  And his feet with the flute and bassoon.

By Heaven! they 're coming this way ;
   And dares she to smile on me still?
Your brother! — what is it you say?
   Your brother — just back from Brazil!

Your pardon! this room has no air —
   Come, walk on the terrace and then —
Ah! sweet is that rose in your hair,
   And I 'm the most blessèd of men.

IN LIBBY.

I HEAR the music of the bells
    Float out upon the summer air —
Now, like the sea their chorus swells,
    Now, faintly, as the breath of prayer;
Yet lingering still as if to bless
    My heart within its loneliness.

The tide comes up from out the bay,
    The sails ride to and fro ;
I stand and watch them all the day,
    Out on the stream below;
But bending sail, nor flowing sea,
    Brings one sweet word of joy to me.

MY VIOLET.

SHE is not here, my violet,
My Maybell sweet, my mignonette,
And so my eyes are often wet, —
She is not here, my violet.

But over there, where ever swells
Each bud and bloom in heavenly dells,
Like nightingale she sings and tells
Our love to the sweet asphodels.

And where the sweet stars ever shine
On jasper seas and hills divine,
I 'll know her by love's constant sign,
And see her still and call her mine.

I hear her to the blossoms hum:
" In the bright days, he, too, will come ; "
And so with eager lips, half dumb,
I only wait that I may come.

It little matters where I be
For a few years, on lake or lea,
For through the gates ajar I see
My brown-haired maid still waiting me.

And sometimes when the stars are set,
And sweet Maybells with dews are wet,
I'll close my eyes and go and get
My brown-haired love, my violet.

THERE IS A MAIDEN WHOM I KNOW.

THERE is a maiden whom I know,
Some sweet six summers old or so;
And to my chair she climbs to throw
  Her soft arms round me lovingly.

There is no maiden in the town .
With lips so red, or hair so brown,
Or cheeks so like the thistle's down,
  Nor one who is so loving me.

Her eyes — bright eyes — I know I dare
To say they are more sweetly rare
Than any others ever were —
  And shine on me so lovingly.

Bright eyes, brown hair, and red lips say
A thousand sweet things every day,
But most, in her dear childish way,
  How very much she 's loving me.

Perhaps *you* know some little miss,
So very sweet and like to this,
Whom every day *you* fondly kiss
   And press to you so lovingly?

It little matters what her name —
If Helen, Kate, or Maud, or Mame,
Sweet child — dear one — 't is all the same,
   Press her and kiss her lovingly.

IN A VINEYARD.

WHEN lads shall clamber 'mid the vines,
And press the purple vintage down,
And maids more rare than Rhenish wines
Shall braid each rustic youth a crown, —
O happy youth! O happy maid!
Who dance to Labor's music chime, —
Well has your poet sweetly said:
"God bless us in the vintage time."

SONG.

THE sea hath its pearls so rare,
  The sky hath its stars so bright,
The river is ever so fair,
  But I have my lover, my light.

Oh! truer than pearls and sea,
  And fairer than stars of night, —
Oh! better than all is he,
  My lover, my dream, my light.

He's coming! I hear, I hear
  The voice of my brave, my knight!
There's joy when his step is near,
  My lover, my dream, my light.

IONE.

Old Surrey's hills are dear to me,
    And Richmond's fields are fair,
And many a bud unfolds its flower
    And leaves a sweetness there, —
But fairest flowers that ever grew,
    Or sweetest bud that 's blown
On Surrey hills will not compare
    With our sweet rose Ione.

The sun was bright the morn she came,
    At least we thought it shone,
And all the birds they seemed to sing
    A welcome to Ione.
The dews that kissed the rose's breast
    The whole sweet night before,
Still lingered for one look at her —
    What could they wish for more?

Ione, Ione, our sweet Ione!
  Our youth renews in thee,
While Surrey's hills and Richmond's fields
  Are very fair to see ;
And Heaven's own doors are opened wide,
  The road has shorter grown ;
Thou bring'st us one step nearer Him,
  Ione, our sweet Ione.

A CENTENNIAL IDYL.

SIX days and nights our gallant ship
Sped o'er a lone and trackless sea;
And we had watched the sea-gulls skip
Like arrows o'er the wave, and dip
Their wings into its foam, while we
Found in their freaks some company.

We were a hundred there, and more
From many lands, yet loved but one;
And we had longed to see the shore,
The first faint mists of Labrador —
To hear some far-off evening gun
Proclaim the day, — the voyage done.

It was so quiet there — at last,
One bolder than the others led:
" Why is this silence?   Let the past
Be of the things that cannot last, —
We are the living — not the dead."
" Give us a song," the captain said.

"Is there none here, not one, not one,
With the divine Promethean fire,
Can sing of deeds most nobly done :
Of sieges lost, of battles won,
Of knightly sons of knightlier sire,
And wake to life the sleeping lyre?

"I do bethink me now, a man
Sat amid the forward decks to-day —
I do not think there ever can
Be one again so old and wan,
As he whose harp beside him lay."
"Bring him," the others said, "to play."

And soon an old man tottered in
To where the lamps were all aglow;
The boatswain bore his harp for him —
For he had thought it well a sin
That one so old should helpless go ;
'T is good we treat our aged so.

"Good friends," the boatswain said, "I bring
The poet of the ship to you,
Well he can play, and sweetly sing
To this, his harp, whose every string

Though tunèd oft, yet, tuned anew,
May cheer you for an hour or two."

. . . .

"Give me the harp," the singer said,
And touched his weird hand to the lyre —
And, lo! the eye that seemed so dead,
The form, whence life had almost fled,
Brightened anew with living fire;
Forgot was age — forgot was pain —
The old man lived the boy again.

He swept the chords through many a strain,
And sung of youth and love, till we,
Like followers in his knightly train,
Wept o'er his touching minstrelsy.
Is it not true that men may be
Made angels by some melody?

Have we not lived, at times, above
The grov'ling earth and its complaints,
On hearing some sweet tale of love,
Some seraph-song of dying saints?
Has not some poet said that we
Are chords in God's great harmony?

. . . .

" Enough — enough ! " the harpist said :
" I sing no more of love's young dream,
Of knightly deeds, of lovers wed,
Of hours, of days, too quickly sped, —
Mine is another, nobler theme —
MY COUNTRY — born midst blood and tears,
Grown sacred by its hundred years.
'T is not so long ago, that men —
Brave men, who feared not storm or sea —
Crossed to the new-born land of Penn,
Without one thought but to be free :
Brave men, good men as well, were they
Who fearless sought the dang'rous way
To Plymouth Rock, to Florida —
Men who could fight, as well as pray,
Nor asked what else their fate might be
In that fair land beyond the sea,
So that it brought them liberty.

" They came — and soon their axes rung
By many a lake and tangled wood ;
And midst their labors, lo ! they sung,
For God was in their solitude.
Their struggles none but He may tell,

Who watched them on their dang'rous way;
How by the lurking foe they fell,
Yet trusted him, and said: ' 'T is well,
He leads us to the coming day.'

" The panther slunk into his lair,
The she-wolf hid within her den,
And there was peace and plenty there,
For God had blessed the hands of men.
Lo! Towns, and States, and Cities rose,
And flocks were fed in every glen, —
It was the bloss'ming of the rose,
For God had blessed the hands of men.

. . . .

" O, would that Peace might ever rest
Her blessed wings on every shore!
Then were mankind divinely blest,
And men should learn of war no more.
Pray, pray, for that good hour in store,
When men shall learn of war no more.

. . . .

"O England! England! tell us where,
Where had we wronged thee? how? or
    when?

Hadst thou forgot thy children there,
Although thy children, yet were men ?
Hadst thou forgot that clime and sea,
And growing years, bring wider range,—
A larger hope, a destiny
That laws or wars can never change ?

" Thy armies came — thy navies flung
Their flag o'er many an inland sea —
And soon the hills of England rung
With shouts and thanks for victory :
With shouts and thanks, but echoing there,
The answer came from swamp and glen,
' You've driven the tiger to his lair —
God help you when he comes again !'

" Towns, cities blazed ; barefooted men
Tramped where our Western rivers flow ;
They left their marks behind them, then,
In bloody lines on frozen snow.
'T was death — aye, more to them, but know
Men oft'nest earn their freedom so.

" Orphans and widows wept in vain,
And armies sank for want of bread ;

Death stalked through every wood and plain,
And fields were left unharvested.
Still would they yield not — No, beware !
God's will is worked through man's despair.

" Days, months, and years, they wavered not,
Nor asked the number of their foe ;
By wounds, by death, they cheaply bought
The rights that tyrants would not know, —
The fairest right — to die to be
The fathers of men's liberty.

" They conquered, and a nation sprung
To life, to greatness, in the West ;
And the wide world her praises sung,
She was the freest and the best ;
She was the freest, and the one
Whose soil no tryant dared to tread —
For, lo ! above, about her, shone
The mystery of her sacred dead.
Fate chose but one — that one was she —
To lead mankind to liberty.

.   .   .   .

" It is a century since then —
A hundred years to-day, and men

Tell all the old tales o'er again ;
How she was born, our land, how bred,
And how the life her children led,
By faith and peace was hallowèd ;
How well she kept her promised vow
To lead the way — to help the oppressed
Of every land and clime, and how
Men worshiped her, and she was blest ;
How commerce came, and all that Fate
Ordains to glorify a State
Waited on her, and she was great ;
Each wind that blew. each sail that bent,
Seemed like some gift divinely sent
To help enrich a continent.
The world was envious, too — but, no !
Kings could not stop what Fate had told ;
Hills, rocks, unbound themselves, and lo !
Their breasts are filled with oil and gold.

.   .   .   .

" What more ?   The land was blest and grew
Like Eden, fair — but never knew
Like it, she nursed a tempter, too.
A tempter — black, fit child of hell —
He came — and half the nation fell.

They fell, and where the daisies grew,
Lo! cannon belched their poisonous breath —
And war her red-mouthed trumpet blew,
And wedding morns saw nights of death.
The hand of Fate lay heavy then,
For God had cursed the ways of men.

"Dark months and years the storm-cloud
    swept
Her course across a widowed land —
But lo! the God of battles kept
The nation in his pitying hand.
At last, at last, the burning smoke
Faded before her silent guns,
But louder than her cannon spoke
The shroudless bodies of her sons.
Weep, fading clouds — speak, silent guns,
And honor these her fallen ones!
Dead was the tempter — dead the past,
And men forgot their burning hate,
For hates and angers cannot last
With men whose foes were good, or great.
Sleep on, ye braves, ye shroudless ones!
Men may not ask which side ye stood;

Enough, ye were the nation's sons,
And ye are dead, and God is good.
It little recks where men have stood,
When Heav'n forgives, and God is good.

"Again the peaceful lilies bloom,
And kiss the graves of friend and foe;
Again, again, the busy loom
Sends its dear music to and fro ;
Again the hills are gold and red,
With shocks and sheaves on every hand,
For all the fields are harvested,
And there is plenty' in the land, —
Plenty and peace, for God again
Has smiled and blessed the hands of men.

" And now, where once the wigwam stood
Upon the Schuylkill's banks of green,
Where redd'ning vines and tangled wood
Hemmed in the fair but dang'rous scene —
Behold! a palace fit for kings
Lifts its fair head unto the skies,
And all the land her tribute brings,
And shouts aloud : ' Friends all, arise, !

This day, this hour, this place must be
Made sacred to men's liberty.'

" And here, where all have met to see
The earth's united rivalry
In all that is, or yet may be,
They reached their hands to each, and said :
' This is the tribute to our dead —
This is the ring with which we wed
The twice-born bride, Columbia —
And this the oath, new-sworn, to thee,
Land of our hopes and destiny.'
Again the old, time-honored scroll,
Whereon the New World's faith was writ,
Was shown to men, and every soul
Thanked God, and wept at sight of it, —
Thanked God, and wept — it was a sight
Such as men see but once in life.
I saw it then — I saw its birth —
What more can one then want on earth ? "

            .   .   .   .

All night our ship sped on its way,
Along a moonlit, starlit sea,
And when the red sun brought the day,

The sailors shouted " Land ! " — and we
Looked to the West, and smiling there
Lay the low hills of Delaware;
Loud fired the guns — the ship-bells rung —
It was the land the poet sung.

Land of the West — our Fatherland !
We bow and greet thee here at sea;
We bare our heads, and meekly stand,
And pray that God in his right hand
May ever keep thee great and free, —
May ever keep thee great, and when,
Th' oppressed shall cry for liberty,
Thy Stars and Stripes shall answer them :
Lo ! here, all men, all men are free.

GYPSY GIRL'S SONG.

THEY 'RE waiting for me in the forest,
  To lead the first reel on the grass :
The hare-bells will spring at my coming,
  The lilies will bow as I pass.

I care not for palace or city,
  My home is the home of the free —
The birds are my playmates in summer,
  My music 's the song of the sea.

All day with my arrows and quiver,
  I wander by meadow and spring ;
And the birds are repeating forever,
  The words of the song that I sing.

THE NATION'S DEAD.

HAIL to the dead — the nation's dead —
 Who sleep by wood and field and shore!
To them we come with loyal tread
 And kneel beside their graves once more.
With notes of bugle-song and drum,
 With flying flags and sweet Mayflowers,
And grateful hearts, again we come
 To deck these soldier graves of ours.

With hopes undimmed by flying years,
 And faith renewed by the great past,
We see amidst our funeral tears
 The glory that was born to last.
Once more beside each verdant grave
 We gather, and with pride recall
How heroes' blood alone could save,
 How heroes' sons alone could fall.

And lifting up the veil of years,
  We hear again the nation's cry —
Its dark distress, its anguished fears,
  Its wail for help — for men to die.
We see the tramping thousands come,
  Their tents shine white on every field;
The nation's heart, it is not dumb,
  It cannot fail, it will not yield.

No longer spears and battle-blades
  To pruning-hooks and staves are bent;
From farms and hills and far-off glades
  The dreadful news is quickly sent;
And sounds of drums and clanging steel
  And braying horns are in the air,
And quick the pulse of men who feel
  Their own heart's blood is flowing there.

And there are partings none may tell,
  And faces paled and lips all dumb,
And broken hearts in one farewell
  To those who go, but never come.
Like to the torrent bounding down
  From some tall mountain to the sea,

From shop and village, farm and town,
  Comes the young nation's chivalry.

And once again is heard the cry
  Of squadrons charging to the death,
And bombs and shells go shrieking by,
  Borne on the red-hot cannon's breath :
And fierce and far o'er Southern fields,
  Like the dread sea to terror blown,
Comes the fierce foe that never yields,
  Or yields to death, and death alone.

On ! on ! we hear the battle's din.
  " On ! on ! " we hear our leader's cry ;
" There is no way but Death's to win " —
  " On ! on ! " the bugles make reply, —
With Farragut among the shrouds,
  Wherever Danger's signals be,
With Hooker fighting in the clouds,
  With Sherman marching to the sea.

" On ! on ! " — we hear them once again
  Shout back the fierce old rebel yell ;
And though from ships and ramparts rain
  The sulphurous smoke, the fire of hell,

Still on, until the withering blast
   Is silenced like the trampled dead,
And fair as morning shines at last
   The Stars and Stripes above their head.

They sleep to-day in silent lines, —
   Heroic men, whom Fame hath lent
The glory that forever shines,
   To be their lasting monument.
And years and men may pass, but they,
   Shrined in their country's bosom, live
In fairer forms than flesh or clay :
   The fitter forms that Fame can give.

Sleep on, sleep on, heroic dead,
   It little recks what we may say,
For there, beyond your narrow bed,
   Shines the new light, your better day ;
And midst the music of the spheres
   That sounds the soldier's reveille,
Where march and countermarch the years,
   Ye wait the Peace that is to be.

ARIADNE.

I WALKED by the yellow Tiber,
  Last night, when the sun was low,
While all in the silent distance
  Grew soft with a purple glow;
And an odor of new-crushed poppies,
  And the smell of the lilies, crept
Deep into my veins, till, weary,
  I lay by the stream and slept.

And stronger the odors pressed me,
  And a dream in my dream there came—
The joy of a love's new greeting,
  Of lips that pronounced my name—
Of a love that was more than mortal,
  Of cheeks that were godly fair;
And I knew that my Dionysius
  Was standing beside me there—

Was standing, his eyes upon me,
  As once, on that other day,

He touched with his wand, and loved me, ·.
  And bore me with him away.
My leopard sprang up to greet him,
  As I waked from the drowsy dream,
With the arms of my new love round me,
  By the side of the Tiber stream.

Oh! come to me, Dionysius—
  I dreamed of the evils by,
When Theseus, false and cursèd,
  Had left me alone to die.
'Twas the poppies that made me dream so,
  And the lilies you love the best—
Oh! kiss me, Dionysius,
  And hold me upon your breast.

And deeper, still deeper, kiss me,
  Nor lessen your warm embrace,
Till our love and our lips commingle,
  Like the blushes upon my face.
Oh! dream of my dream, I have you;
  Look out from your coal-black eyes,
For the light and the love they give me
  Were born of a Paradise.

Push back the curls from your forehead,
  And your cheek, be it close to mine,
Till our hearts beat warm together,
  As our arms each other entwine.
There, breathe in my soul one moment,
  For the touch of thy lips is worth
A thousand of mortal's kisses—
  An age of the loves of earth.

Oh! life of my life, come near me,
  Look into my eyes again,
And closer, oh! closer press me,
  For the love that is born of pain ;
I swoon, but my eyes are open—
  I faint, but I see thy face—
Oh! happiness, born to woman,
  To be in a god's embrace.

Come on to the sweet flute's playing,
  The feet that are drunk with dance,
The loves, and the bacchant women,
  Who die, if without thy glance ;
Lead on by the gardens blowing,
  By the meadows of sweet perfume,

For where thy light breath toucheth,
  The beautiful roses bloom.

Look ! look at the dancers coming,
  The train and the festal wine,
The pans and the satyrs leading,
  The buds and the blossomed vine.
Thus, thus, I will be immortal,
  My name in the bright stars set,
With the marriage-crown you gave me
  The day that our kisses met.

NOTES.

Sherman's March to the Sea.

This song, which has the honor of giving its name to the most picturesque campaign of the War, "The March to the Sea," and was characterized by General Sherman himself as the shortest complete history of the same, was written one chilly morning in a little wedge tent at the rebel prison camp of Columbia, S. C., where Adjutant Byers had the hard fate to be quartered, with some hundreds of fellow-prisoners. Meagre reports of Sherman's leaving Atlanta had come through a daily rebel paper, which a kindly disposed negro stuffed into the loaf of bread furnished to a mess of the Union prisoners who were fortunate enough to have a little money to pay for it. Through its troubled lines the eager ears and eyes of the starved men read hope and coming freedom.

Another prisoner, Lieutenant Rockwell, heard the poem and under the floor of the hospital building, where a number of musical prisoners quartered themselves on mother earth, wrote the music. It was first sung by the prison glee club, led by Major Isett, where, intermingled with the strains of "Dixie" and kindred airs, to adapt it to rebel hearers, it was heard with applause. By the fortune of war, the entry of General Sherman's victorious army into Columbia released Adjutant Byers from a fifteen months' captivity. General Sherman gave him a temporary position on his staff, and, later, sent him as the bearer of the first despatches North to General Grant and President Lincoln, announcing the victorious progress of his army through the Carolinas.

On reaching the North, Adjutant Byers was astonished to hear that his verses had preceded him, and had become popular as a song all over the country. The song assumes the march to have commenced at Chattanooga, not Atlanta, and it is now well known that Sherman's hard-fought Atlanta campaign was by him intended as the first step for the ocean.

The Ballad of Columbus.

The fates seem to have conspired in making the life of Columbus romantic as well as great. There is not an incident mentioned in the ballad that does not find its authority in sober history. From the sudden eruption of the volcano on Teneriffe to the death scene in a little unknown Seville inn, each step of the voyager's life was as if done in a drama.

The dearest wish of Columbus had been to secure great sums of money in the New World, to be used in equipping an army for the rescue of the Holy Sepulchre.

Margery Brown.

The London *Lancet* relates how a young girl, losing her lover, became insane, and lost all calculation of time. She never knew that she was growing older, and, believing herself always young, remained so in appearance, and at seventy was as blooming as a girl of twenty. Her case was a psychological marvel, cited to prove the influence of the mind over the body.

News at the White House.

During the battle of Chattanooga President Lincoln sat alone at a telegraph instrument listening to the great news as it was wired up to Washington. The assault, in which the writer took part, commenced as soon as Sherman's troops had crossed the Tennessee River at Chickamauga Creek.

The Guard on the Volga.

Some years since, when the terrible plague was devastating parts of Asia. the Russians established a line of pickets along the Volga River to incercept travel, and thus check the march of the disease into their country.

The Tramp of Sherman's Army.

Recited at the reunion of the Army of the Tennessee in Cincinnati, September 26, 1889.   General Sherman presided.   All the then living generals of the great Army of the Tennessee were on the stage, and participated. The toasts for the occasion were printed on beautiful satin maps representing Sherman's greatest campaign, and their sentiments consisted of extracts and parts of verses from the Lyric of "Sherman's March to the Sea."

It was General Sherman's last public appearance as President of the Society that comprised nearly all the officers who had marched and fought with him from Chattanooga to the ocean.

The Nation's Dead.

Written for, and recited at, the Decoration Day Services in Washington City, 1881.

President Garfield was one of the participants.